"*I want to place just one brick in the structure that makes up [the listener's] life. That's really what a podcast is all about.*"

~ Jordan Harbinger, Host of *The Jordan Harbinger Show*

TO ALL THOSE WILLING TO SHARE THEIR KNOWLEDGE SO GENEROUSLY, IMPACTING OUR LIVES SO PROFOUNDLY. THANK YOU.

Published by LHC Publishing 2020

Daddy Is A Podcast Host
Text Copyright © 2020 Y. Eevi Jones
Illustrations Copyright © 2020 Y. Eevi Jones

Printed in the USA.
All rights reserved.
No part of this book may be reproduced in any form without the written permission of the copyright holder.

All inquiries should be directed to
www.LHCpublishing.com

ISBN-13: 978-1-7323733-9-6 Hardcover
ISBN-13: 978-1-7323733-8-9 Paperback

My Daddy is a Podcast Host

A Podcast Book For Kids

Eevi Jones

A tap-tap and "One, two!"
I hear from the base of our house.
The 'RECORDING' light's flashing.
I'm as quiet as a mouse...
(not)

Behind that door's the room
daddy has claimed for his show
he records every week
with folks others all ought to know.

A pressed shirt up top,
looking polished and neat.
His bottoms are missing,
and quite sockless his feet.

"**Welcome to the show,**" he shouts and cheers into the mic, for when on air, he's filled with thrill and elation so bright.

Decoding stories and secrets, skills and much more, of wisdom-filled people that he feels the need to explore.

Virtual meetings set up
via screen, cam, and web.
Guest and host come together
to converse and to chat.

"Tell me more," daddy'd say,
his interest hooked with intent.
Leaning in, learning more
from his newfound friend.

From his guest that,
through many phases and hues,
has learned a few lessons
of great value and use.

People's grand wisdom
daddy turns into solid advice
that listeners can use
to truly **impact their lives**.

Each guest's stories and thoughts,
too grand to ignore.
Leaving everyone better
than they had been before.

Through earbuds and headphones,
speakers and more,
listeners binge and consume,
tune in, and explore.

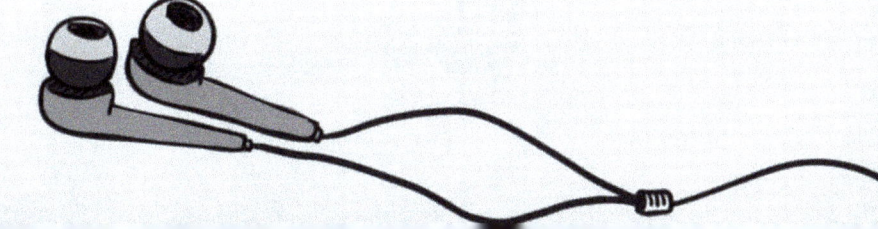

Daddy's audience, subscribers, followers, fans, hit play while they drive, lift weights, sit on trains.

Show notes aplenty,
sponsors announced and shared,
provide a show free for all,
where all costs are spared.

Reaching hundreds of thousands
of those hungry for more.
All from daddy's basement,
his **sockless feet** tap-tapping the floor.

We can build castles with Legos.
We can build them with sand.
Daddy builds his with knowledge,
always ready to forever expand.

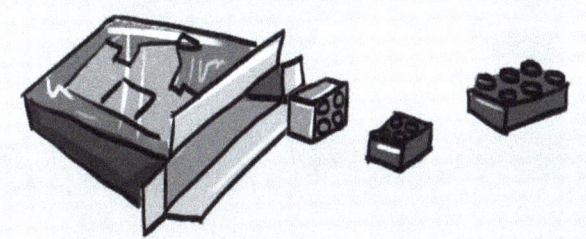

Digging deep wells of friendships,
webbing a net throughout life.
For by connecting with others,
we truly grow, rise, and thrive.

Making a difference, an impact
- that's daddy's life's goal.
Helping others advance, excel,
and to take full control.

Goodbyes and farewells.
The podcast's all done.
I can't wait for daddy
to soon host his very next one.

I'll be just like daddy,
when I'm big and all grown.
I'll help others to learn
through a show of my own.

With elation, full heart,
and a smile so bright,
fulfilled and quite happy,
daddy turns off his mic.

One brick at a time,
that's how all structures gain might.
And today, daddy placed yet another
into a listener's life.

The End

This ~~episode~~ was produced by...
       ^book

PODCASTS THAT HAVE HAD A PROFOUND IMPACT ON MY LIFE

From the bottom of my heart - thank you!

- THE CREATIVE PENN
- SCHOOL OF GREATNESS
- DON'T KEEP YOUR DAY JOB
- SO MONEY
- FRESH AIR
- THE SUNNY SHOW
- RADIOLAB
- THE SELF PUBLISHING SHOW
- THE UNMISTAKABLE CREATIVE
- SMART PASSIVE INCOME
- PHILOSOPHIZE THIS!
- CAR TALK
- THE JORDAN HARBINGER SHOW
- THE RICHIE NORTON SHOW
- FREAKONOMICS RADIO
- STUFF YOU SHOULD KNOW
- HOW I BUILT THIS
- SCREW THE NINE TO FIVE
- ENTREPRENEUR ON FIRE
- EARN YOUR HAPPY
- GOAL DIGGER
- HIDDEN BRAIN
- WAIT WAIT...DON'T TELL ME!
- REVISIONIST HISTORY
- THE TIM FERRISS SHOW
- THE BOOK MARKETING SHOW
- DECONSTRUCTING SUCCESS

ABOUT THE AUTHOR

Writing under a number of pen names, Y. Eevi Jones is an award-winning & bestselling children's book author, and the founder of Children's Book University™. She was born in former East Germany to a German mother and a Vietnamese father. Thus, she spent an inordinate amount of her youth nosing through books that she shouldn't have been reading, and watching movies that she shouldn't have been watching. It was a good childhood.

Always drawing inspiration from her own two children, she loves to write about unique interests and aspires to find fun and exciting ways to have kids discover and learn about the magnificent marvels this world has to offer.

Eevi has been featured in Forbes, Scary Mommy, Huffington Post, Exceptional Parent Magazine, SCBWI, and many more.

She can be found online at **www.BravingTheWorldBooks.com**.

A WORD BY THE AUTHOR

If you enjoyed this book, it would be wonderful if you could take a short minute to leave a lovely review on Amazon, as your kind feedback is very appreciated and so very important. It gives me, the author, encouragement for bad days when I want to take up scorpion petting. Thank you so very much for your time!

BRAVING THE WORLD™ SERIES

AWARD-WINNING SERIES

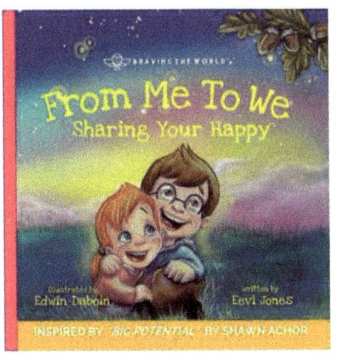
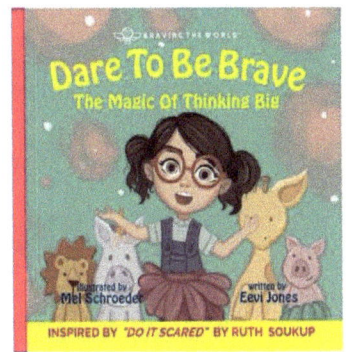
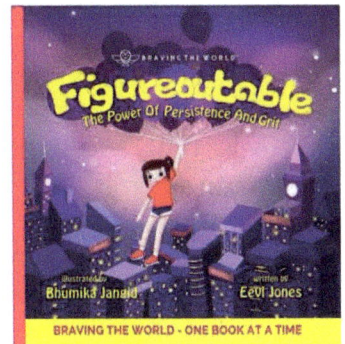

... AND MORE

OTHER WORKS BY THIS AUTHOR

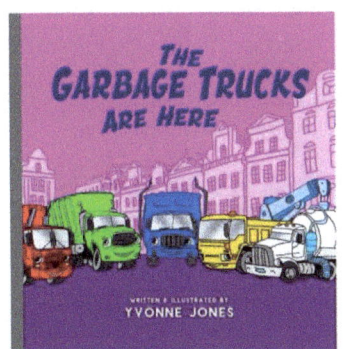
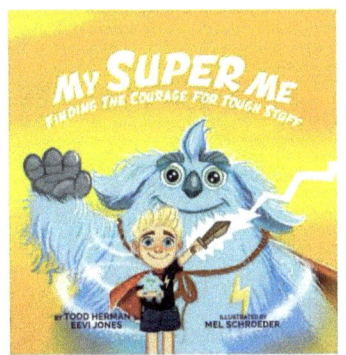
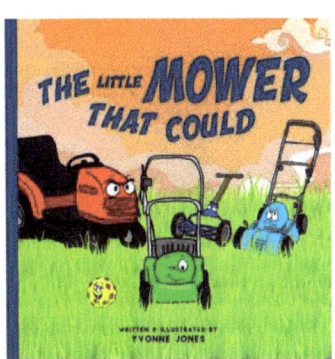
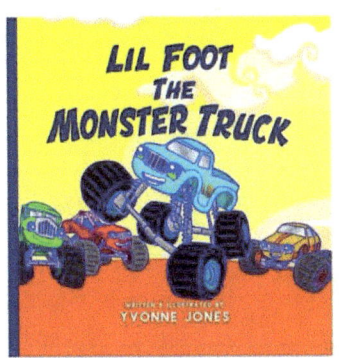
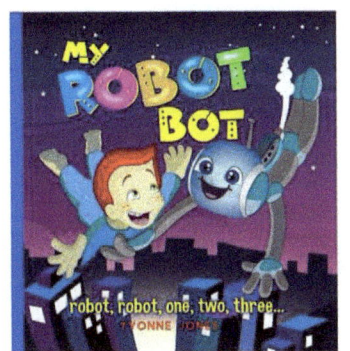
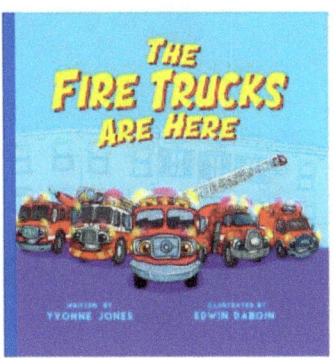

www.BravingTheWorldBooks.com

Printed in the USA
CPSIA information can be obtained
at www.ICGtesting.com
LVHW082325220923
759028LV00025B/26